Foursome the Spider

Written by **LARRY NESTOR** and Illustrated by **MICHAEL GLENN MONROE**

Sleeping Bear Press
310 North Main Street
P.O. Box 20
Chelsea, MI 48118
www.sleepingbearpress.com

Printed and bound in Canada.

10 9 8 7 6 5 4 3 2 1

Library of Congress Cataloging-in-Publication Data

Nestor, Larry.
Foursome the spider / by Larry Nestor.
p. cm.
Summary: The inhabitants of an insect museum get along very well but
keep to their own areas until a spider, recently removed from a golf
course, involves them all in his favorite pastime.
ISBN 1-58536-079-1
[1. Spiders—Fiction. 2. Insects—Fiction. 3. Golf—Fiction. 4.
Toleration—Fiction. 5. Museums—Fiction.] I. Title.
PZ7.N43855 Fo 2001
[Fic]—dc21
—2001005421

To Irene

Larry Nestor

❧

To my grandfather, who taught me the game.

Michael Glenn Monroe

In a not-too-big city not far from a beautiful lake was a nature center. Within the nature center there was one large, glass room filled with plants, trees, and even a narrow stream. Amid the plants and stream lived ants from Africa, bees from Brazil, butterflies from Belgium, crickets from Chile, fireflies from France, grasshoppers from Greece, and a few not-so-familiar insects. The glass-enclosed room was quiet and peaceful. Ants played happily on their anthills, dragonflies floated on deep green lily pads, and butterflies played hide-and-seek in the colorful bushes. Deidre, the caretaker, made sure all living there knew the main rule: *Kindness and Consideration for All.* It was painted over the main doorway. Everyone lived peacefully in their own area.

Because the bugs came from so many different parts of the world, visitors to the center were surprised at how the bugs got along so well. One little girl remarked, "They are simply obeying the sign." Indeed, it was surprising how the butterflies and insects tended to remain in their own small areas, never invading the privacy of others.

Then along came a large spider. He was silver-gray with fuzzy legs and had argyle-like markings of red, green, blue, and yellow on his body. He had been living at a nearby golf course. His home was in the 18th hole. Because of his unusual markings and his unusual home, golfers had nicknamed him Foursome. They had come to like Foursome but they all realized that it would be safer for Foursome to move to the nature center. Deidre, the caretaker, who played golf at this golf course, offered to take Foursome to his new home.

Once inside the nature center's large, glass room, Foursome found an empty corner and built his web. Afterward, he collected a tiny twig and several small seeds. He used the twig to knock the seeds back and forth, being careful to stay in the area below his web.

Bright and early the next morning, Deidre came to check on Foursome. He was still busy swinging the twig at the seeds. Pretending to hold a golf club, Deidre took a couple of practice swings herself, noting that it was the first time she had ever seen a spider smile.

Deidre then watched with fascination as Foursome passed the twig to a different pair of his legs and hit another seed. Upon seeing this, Deidre quickly ran to her office and excitedly phoned the local newspaper.

A reporter and a photographer immediately drove to the nature center, and the next day the paper carried a photo of the spider along with a story under a headline that read NATURE CENTER'S NEWEST RESIDENT, FOURSOME THE SPIDER, GOLFS! By midmorning there was a long line of people forming, anxious to see the spider.

Foursome soon grew tired of remaining in his corner and longed to venture out into unknown regions of the glass room. He decided to hit his seed just a little farther past his web. Foursome lined up his shot, took a deep breath, and hit the seed into an area of tall grass.

He wanted to share the fun and excitement of the game of golf with the other insects, but was afraid of offending them.

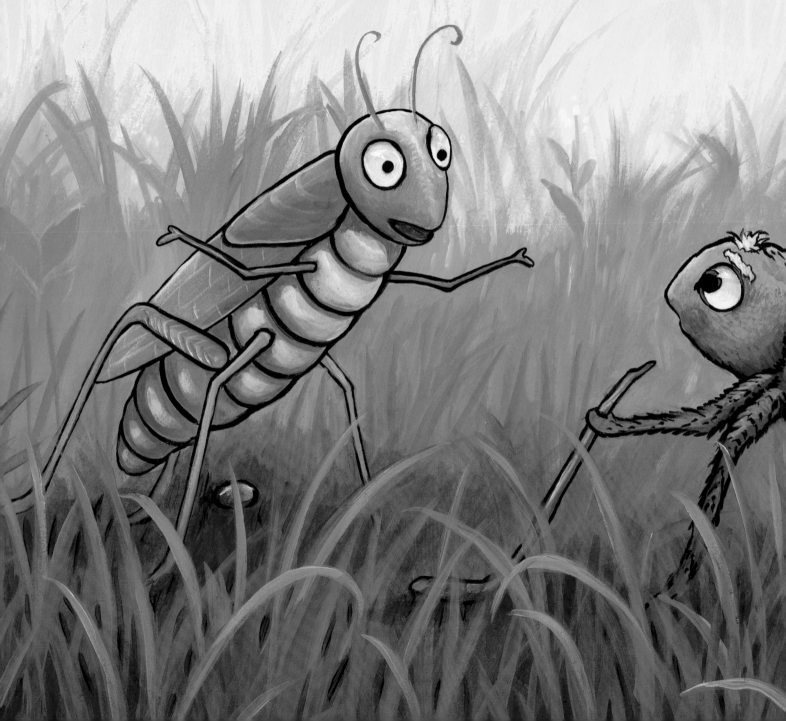

As Foursome pushed his way through the tall grass, he disturbed a sleeping grasshopper who awoke and jumped a foot in the air upon realizing a spider was in his space.

"What are you doing here?" shouted the grasshopper.

"I'm looking for my lost golf seed," replied Foursome.

"That's the silliest thing I've ever heard," grumbled the grasshopper. "Only people play golf."

"I learned the game from them and now I'm a golfer too," said Foursome proudly.

"Would you mind coming along and being my caddie?" asked Foursome. "Every golfer needs a helper and you could help me find my golf seed and learn about the game of golf at the same time. I am heading for the big tree."

Always interested in an adventure, the grasshopper agreed to assist Foursome and they found the seed in the tall grass. A grateful Foursome then took his next shot.

As they moved along a narrow meadow searching for the seed, they could see several large anthills ahead of them. It was there that Foursome found his golf seed resting halfway up one of the hills.

As Foursome walked up and down the anthill trying to decide how to play the next shot, several ants emerged from the entrance.

"Just what do you think you're doing?" asked an angry ant.

"I just moved here and I'm playing golf," was the spider's response.

"I do not know what the rules of golf are but I do know you are in our area. I'll forgive you this time since you're new here, but I don't expect it to happen again," stated the ant.

"Thank you and I'm very sorry we disturbed you," said Foursome. "I was trying to hit my seed more to the left."

"Well, carry on then," responded the ant with a hint of curiosity in his voice.

The ants watched as Foursome hit a long, high shot that narrowly missed the lower branches of a bush filled with butterflies. Sensing the danger, the butterflies flew off the bush, filling the air with color.

"Sorry butterflies," said Foursome. "I'll watch out for you next time."

Taking another swing, he was on his way again.

Soon they came to a stream filled with lily pads.

"Those lily pads are reserved for dragon-flies," warned an anxious ant. We're not allowed on them."

"Do you think you can hit it over the water?" asked the grasshopper.

"I hope so," replied Foursome.

"You probably could use a longer twig," advised the grasshopper.

He quickly hopped about and found one. "Here, try this."

Foursome hit the golf seed, hoping it would cross over the water but the golf seed fell onto a lily pad in the center of the stream.

"Oh no! Now what do I do?" asked Foursome. "How am I going to hit my next shot from there?"

"Those dragonflies aren't going to be very happy about this," said the ant. "They can get pretty upset."

"I'll help you," said a butterfly. Foursome crawled onto the butterfly's back and they flew to where a group of dragonflies were discussing the matter. Foursome apologized and asked for permission to play on.

The butterfly was given permission to land on the lily pad, from which Foursome played a remarkable recovery shot to the other side of the stream. The dragonflies, not wanting to miss any of the excitement, offered to carry the other insects across the water, saying, "This golf game is great fun. And the spider is so friendly and polite, maybe sometime he will teach us to play."

"I agree!" cheered an enthusiastic ant. "I think we should all learn the game. Maybe we can invite insects from all over to join us."

"Quiet, please," said Foursome. "This is a tough shot. I really need to stay focused."

"What are you trying to do?" asked the grasshopper.

"I want to shoot over the clump of moss and between the two flowers, but I don't know what's on the other side of the moss."

"That's my job," responded the grasshopper, jumping his way to the top of the moss. Momentarily, the grasshopper returned. "There are three ladybugs having a tea party on a mushroom. I told them to duck under the mushroom until after you take your shot."

Foursome scorched a shot hoping that he had avoided the area where the ladybugs were having their tea.

But when Foursome reached the top of the moss he was confronted by three rather upset ladybugs. "Sir, did you do that on purpose?"

"I hit the golf seed on purpose," replied Foursome.

"Your golf seed struck our mushroom, toppling our teapot and tea cups, spilling our tea, and ruining our party."

"Madam, I assure you that was not my intention," pleaded Foursome.

"Well, you were way off," chimed the ladybugs.

A tear started to form in Foursome's eye.

"There's really no reason to be so upset," said one of the young ladybugs. "They're just dishes and no one was hurt. Besides, it appears you are all having so much fun together. For so long we've all remained in our own little areas. You brought us together, my good spider. You have also shown us, through the game of golf, that we can play in all the areas of the nature center and still be kind and courteous to one another. Now, let's find that seed."

The butterflies and insects cheered their approval as they joined in the search for Foursome's golf seed.

Just then, a large cloud came over the glass room, casting a huge shadow within the room making it difficult to see the golf seed. Fortunately, a squadron of fireflies was nearby and they aimed their light to help the others find the seed. Everyone cheered and the game continued.

The most memorable shot of the day came when Foursome's golf seed became lodged in the fork of a branch near the top of a shrub. Foursome climbed to a higher branch and lowered himself down on a single strand of spun web.

In a flash, Foursome swung and struck a powerful blow to the golf seed, sending it through plants and shrubs and landing it just one short shot from the tree.

For a moment silence fell over the gallery, soon followed by thundering applause and shouts of praise as Foursome lined up his final shot.

Within a week, all of the bugs in the nature center were having Foursome teach them how to play golf. Grasshopper was appointed the greenkeeper. He was in charge of keeping the bunkers raked and fairways trimmed. Grasshopper never had trouble finding enough hungry insects to keep the fairway grass nibbled down to proper length.

The media fondly refers to Foursome as "the Golf Bug." Mothers, fathers, and children from all around come to watch "the Golf Bug" and all of his friends having fun playing golf while showing kindness and consideration to all.

Larry Nestor

When Larry was in second grade he requested a typewriter for Christmas, but he did not begin his professional career until he was 22. A writer/songwriter/musician, he has written lyrics and music for many musicals, and nearly one thousand songs including "Whiz Me A Frisbee!" (Captain Kangaroo) and "We Play Baseball!" (Nickelodeon). He is a member of the American Society of Composers, Authors, and Publishers and the American Federation of Musicians. He has a son, Tom, and a daughter, Anne.

Michael Glenn Monroe

Illustrator Michael Monroe's first painting was of a snow-white winter mink. His father later teased him that he'd drawn "the skinniest polar bear" he'd ever seen. Undaunted, Michael honed his craft through the years, teaching himself new techniques, becoming a renowned wildlife artist and the winner of the 1997 Michigan Duck Stamp award. His first two children's books, *M is for Mitten: A Michigan Alphabet* and *Buzzy the bumblebee*, took him to schools throughout the state, teaching schoolchildren simple shapes and techniques they can use to begin drawing. Christmas 2000, he released the bestseller, *A Wish to be a Christmas Tree*, written by his wife, Colleen. Michael has been selected to paint the 2002 National Easter Egg. The Monroes reside in Brighton, Michigan with their twins, Matthew and Natalie and new baby, John.